Bear's Merry Book of Hidden Things

GERGELY DUDÁS

HARPER
An Imprint of HarperCollinsPublishers

To Móni, who always believed in me

HarperCollins

Bear's Merry Book of Hidden Things
Copyright © 2017 by Gergely Dudás
All rights reserved. Manufactured in China.
No part of this book may be used or reproduced in any manner whatsoever without written
permission except in the case of brief quotations embodied in critical articles and reviews.
For information address HarperCollins Children's Books,
a division of HarperCollins Publishers, 195 Broadway, New York, NY 10007.
www.harpercollinschildrens.com

Library of Congress Control Number: 2016958067
ISBN 978-0-06-257078-9

Typography by Alison Klapthor
17 18 19 20 21 SCP 10 9 8 7 6 5 4 3 2 1
❖
First Edition

This is Bear. He invited all his friends to a very special holiday party.

But then Bear lost track of time . . . and now Christmas is almost here!

"Oh dear," says Bear. "How can I possibly find everything before the party tonight?"

Can YOU help Bear get ready?

What does Bear need first?

Everyone knows a party is better with music!

Maybe Bear can find a **horn**

at this Christmas market.

A jolly **gingerbread man** will certainly bring

some holiday cheer!

Can Bear spot one in this crowd of gingerbread cookies?

Wrapping gifts is half the fun of giving them—

but Bear missed one!

Do you spy an **unwrapped box** in this batch?

Now Bear wants a card to go with his gift.

Help him track down a fun **holiday card**

in this stack of shopping bags!

A party host should always look his best, Bear thinks.

Most of these hats aren't festive enough, though.

Do you see a red **Santa hat** in the flock?

Bear's excited! He can't wait to show his friends

the skating pond behind his house.

But he lost his **ice skate** among all these boots.

Now it's time for decorations! Bear wants to hang a

Christmas stocking by the fireplace.

But the stocking he likes is mixed in with all these mittens!

It would be very merry to decorate my house with a wreath! Bear thinks.

Now all he has to do is find one!

Can you see a **wreath** among the Christmas trees?

A big **red bow** would sure look nice on Bear's door!

Hmm, it's awfully hard to spot one among

all these festive flowers. . . .

How can Bear make the party extra jolly?

By hanging some holly around the house, of course!

Can you glimpse any **holly leaves** in this tangle of garlands?

Twinkly lights make Bear smile, but a golden

jingle bell would really add the perfect touch.

Pinecones would fit the party's woodsy winter theme.

But Bear can't see any among these happy hedgehogs!

Could a **pinecone** be hiding here?

Phew! All the decorations are done!

Now, if Bear finds a **sled**, his friends can slide down the hill behind his house.

Can you help him locate one in this

winter wonderland?

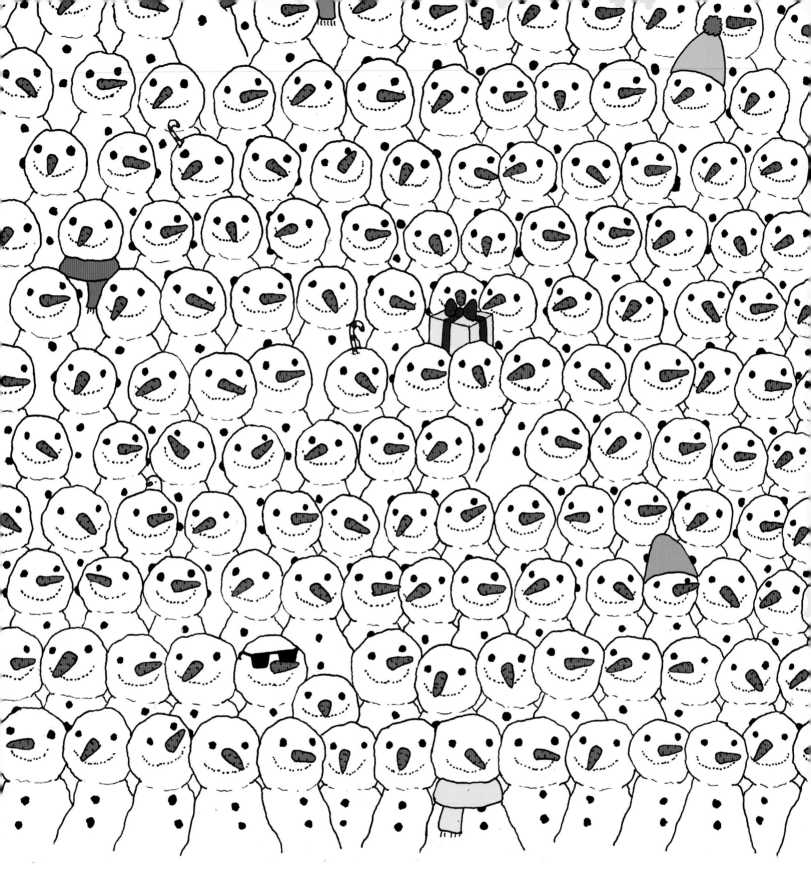

It wouldn't feel like the holidays without a traditional **turtledove**!

But Bear can't seem to spy the shy bird hiding

among all these snowmen. . . .

Oh dear! Bear's getting thirsty from all this hard work!

His penguin friends have a **mug of hot cocoa** for him—

but where?

Now Bear has a bright idea:

a **Christmas candle** to light up the night!

His owl friends might be hiding one somewhere. . . .

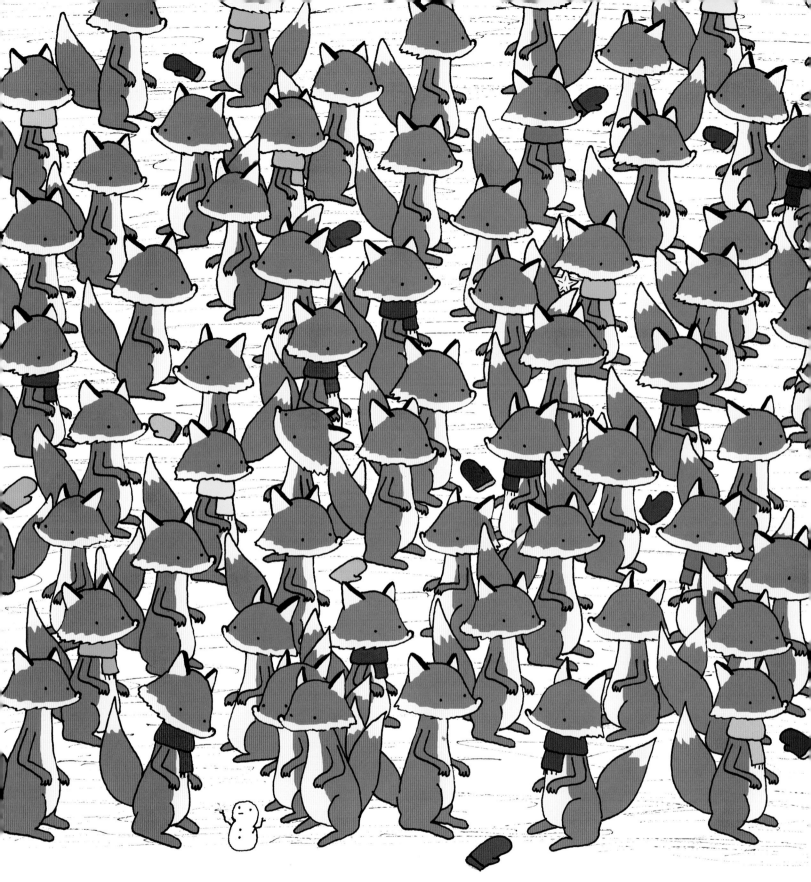

Bear remembers that a Christmas tree always looks best

with a **sparkly star** on top.

Maybe these foxy foxes can help him find one!

Oh no! Look what time it is! Bear must get home soon.
But he still needs some sweet treats from the candy factory.

To start, let's try to find a **holiday lollipop**.

Can you spot one?

Bear has almost enough ornaments.

He just needs one more to finish his tree.

A cheery **red glass ball** would be perfect—is there one here?

These tasty cakes would delight all of Bear's guests.

Could there also be a rum-pa-pum-pum

Christmas drum among them?

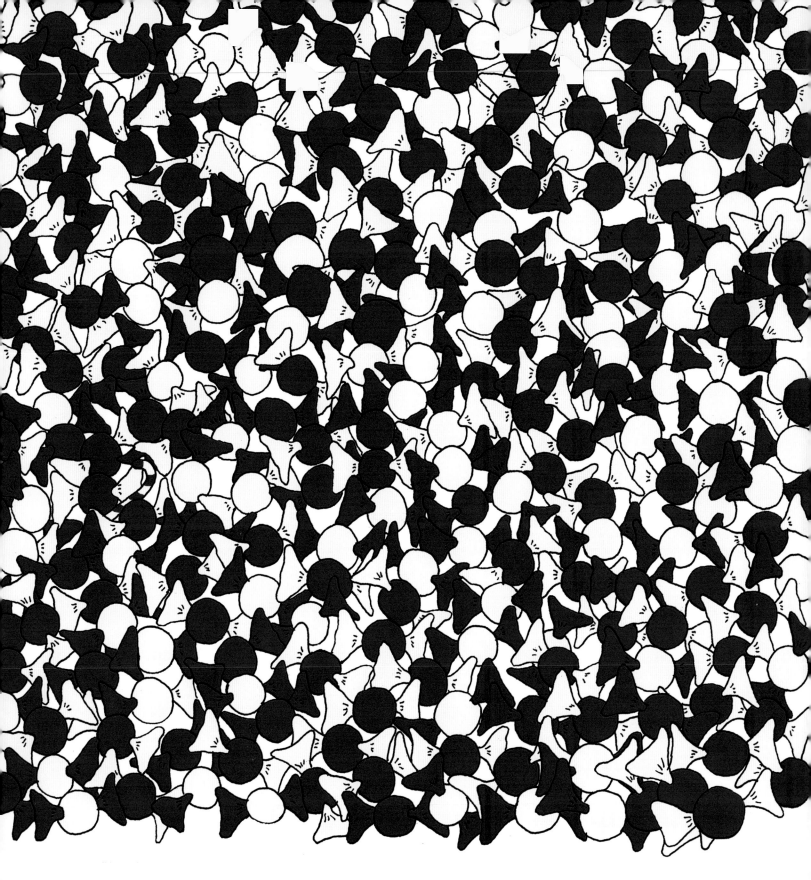

Bear knows that no holiday is complete

without a **candy cane**!

Where could one be hiding?

Last but not least, Bear decides a **peppermint**

would make his dessert table perfect.

There might be one snuggled in among these cupcakes. . . .

Now it's party time!

And Bear couldn't have done it without you!

He's so happy to be celebrating with all his friends!

(Have you seen any of them before?)

Happy holidays, Bear!